THE RISING

MORE SELECTED SCENES FROM THE END OF THE WORLD

BRIAN KEENE

DEATH'S HEAD PRESS

Published by Death's Head Press,
an imprint of Dead Sky Publishing, LLC
Miami Beach, Florida
www.deadskypublishing.com

Edited by Deanna Destito

Paperback ISBN: 9781639511839
eBook ISBN: 9781639512041

PRAISE FOR BRIAN KEENE

"A virtuoso writer. A true master of the genre."
— *FANGORIA*

"If Brian Keene's books were music, they would occupy a working-class, hard-earned space between Bruce Springsteen, Eminem, and Johnny Cash." — JOHN SKIPP

"Try *Darkness On the Edge of Town* by Brian Keene. Excellent short horror novel." — STEPHEN KING

"The enormity of Keene's pulp horror imagination, and his success in bringing the reader over the top with him, is both rare and wonderful." — *PUBLISHERS WEEKLY*

"For over two decades, author Brian Keene has given fans stories filled with zombies, massive man-eating earthworms, an occult detective, a well-meaning serial killer, and numerous other tales of horror, dark fantasy and crime fiction." — *BLOODY DISGUSTING*

"Brian Keene writes the best sort of horror—human, honest, and terrifying." — CHRISTOPHER GOLDEN

"*End of the Road* is one of the very best books about the life of a writer that I have ever read." — KIT POWER

"*The Complex* is a full-throttle action ride... a beautifully developed character study filtered through the lens of viscera and violence." — *NIGHT WORMS*

"*The Last Zombie* series is an intense tale about humanity's fate post-zombie apocalypse and exemplifies Keene's taste for darker, action-oriented tales." — *BLEEDING COOL*

"The man made a huge name for himself with the publication of his first novel, the zombie epic *The Rising*. This was one of those books that everyone was talking about, and for once it actually lived up to the hype. The traditional zombie apocalypse story with some incredibly fresh new elements and great characters made it a fantastic debut." — *DREAD CENTRAL*

"The *Clickers* series is a must-read for fans of horror and science fiction." — *THE HORROR REVIEW*

"Brian Keene revitalized the horror genre."
  — *THE SUFFOLK JOURNAL*

"More power to Brian Keene! He reminds us that horror fiction can deal with fear, not just indulge it."
  — RAMSEY CAMPBELL

"Hoping for a good night's sleep? Stay away from *The Rising*. It'll keep you awake, then fill your dreams with hungry, lurching corpses." — RICHARD LAYMON

"Brian Keene has forever raised the bar for extreme horror." — GARY A. BRAUNBECK

"Not for the squeamish!" — *LIBRARY JOURNAL*

"Brian Keene writes like a force of nature."
— F. PAUL WILSON

ALSO BY BRIAN KEENE

NON-SERIES:

Alone ~ An Occurrence in Crazy Bear Valley ~ The Cage ~
Castaways ~ The Complex ~ The Damned Highway *(with Nick
Mamatas)* ~ Darkness on the Edge of Town ~ Dead Sea ~
Dissonant Harmonies *(with Bev Vincent)* ~ Entombed ~ Ghoul ~
The Girl on the Glider ~ Island of the Dead ~ Jack's Magic Beans
~ Kill Whitey ~ Monsters of Saipan *(with Weston Ochse)* ~
Nemesai *(with John Urbancik)* ~ Pressure ~ School's Out ~ Scratch
~ Shades *(with Geoff Cooper)* ~ Silverwood: The Door *(with Richard
Chizmar, Stephen Kozeniewski, Michelle Garza and Melissa Lason)* ~
Sixty-Five Stirrup Iron Road *(with Edward Lee, Jack Ketchum, J.F.
Gonzalez, Bryan Smith, Wrath James White, Nate Southard, Ryan
Harding, and Shane McKenzie)* ~ Take the Long Way Home ~
Tequila's Sunrise ~ Terminal ~ Thor: Metal Gods *(with Aaron
Stewart-Ahn, Yoon Ha Lee and Jay Edidin)* ~ White Fire ~ With
Teeth

THE RISING SERIES:

The Rising ~ City of the Dead ~ The Rising: Selected Scenes From
the End of the World ~ The Rising: Deliverance

THE EARTHWORM GODS SERIES:

Earthworm Gods *(also published as* The Conqueror Worms*)* ~
Earthworm Gods II: Deluge ~ Earthworm Gods: Selected Scenes
From the End of the World

THE LEVI STOLTZFUS SERIES:

Dark Hollow ~ Ghost Walk ~ A Gathering of Crows ~ Last of the
Albatwitches ~ Invisible Monsters

THE LABYRINTH SERIES:

The Seven ~ Submerged ~ Splintered ~ Falling Angels

THE CLICKERS SERIES *(with J.F. Gonzalez)*:

Clickers II: The Next Wave ~ Clickers III: Dagon Rising ~ Clickers vs. Zombies

THE LOST LEVEL SERIES:

The Lost Level ~ Return To the Lost Level ~ Hole In the World ~ Beneath the Lost Level

THE ROGAN SERIES *(with Steven L. Shrewsbury)*:

King of the Bastards ~ Throne of the Bastards ~ Curse of the Bastards

THE GOTHIC SERIES:

Urban Gothic ~ Suburban Gothic *(with Bryan Smith)*

NON-FICTION:

End of the Road ~ The Triangle of Belief ~ Trigger Warnings ~ Unsafe Spaces ~ Other Words ~ Love and Hate in the Time of Covid ~ Sundancing ~ Sympathy For the Devil: The Best of Hail Saten Vol. 1 ~ Running With the Devil: The Best of Hail Saten Vol. 2 ~ The New Fear: The Best of Hail Saten Vol. 3 ~ Leader of the Banned: The Best of Hail Saten Vol. 4

COLLECTIONS:

Blood on the Page: The Complete Short Fiction, Vol. 1 ~ All Dark, All the Time: The Complete Short Fiction, Vol. 2 ~ Love Letters From A Nihilist: The Complete Short Fiction, Vol 3 ~ Where We Live and Die ~ A Little Silver Book of Streetwise Stories ~ 4X4 *(with Geoff Cooper, Michael Oliveri, and Michael T. Huyck Jr.)* ~ No Rest For The Wicked ~ No Rest At All ~ Fear of Gravity ~ Unhappy Endings ~ A Conspiracy of One ~ The Cruelty of Autumn ~ Good Things For Bad People ~ A Little Sorrowed Talk ~ Stories For the Next Pandemic ~ Things Left Behind *(with Mary SanGiovanni)*

GRAPHIC NOVELS:

The Last Zombie: Dead New World ~ The Last Zombie: Inferno ~ The Last Zombie: Neverland ~ The Last Zombie: Before the After

~ The Last Zombie: The End ~ Dead of Night: Devil-Slayer ~ He-Man and the Masters of the Universe: Origins of Eternia ~ A Very DC Halloween ~ DC House of Horror ~ Gwendy's Button Box ~ The Fallen

MISCELLANY:

Apocrypha ~ The Rising: Death In Four Colors ~ A Field Guide To the Thirteen *(with Mark Sylva)* ~ Liber Nigrum Scientia Secreta *(with J.F. Gonzalez)* ~ Terminal: The Play *(with Roy C. Booth)*

OMNIBUSES:

LeHorn's Hollow ~ The Last Zombie ~ The Last Zombie: Reskinned

AS EDITOR:

The End of the World As We Know It: Tales of Stephen King's The Stand *(with Christopher Golden)* ~ Clickers Forever: A Tribute to J.F. Gonzalez ~ The Drive-In: Multiplex *(with Christopher Golden)* ~ The Best of Horrorfind ~ The Best of Horrorfind II ~ Operation Ice Bat ~ In Delirium ~ New Dark Visions 2 ~ New Dawn ~ The Daughters of Inanna

This one is for Kristopher Triana and Bear...

ACKNOWLEDGMENTS

My sincere thanks to Jeremy Wagner and Steve Wands;
Charlie Benante; Wes Benscoter, Corey Babcock, Andy and
Sirena Martin, Alexander Bailey, Anthony Naylor,
Benjamin Baca, Megan Bini, Jason Adams, Sabas Moreno,
and Sadie Hartmann; Kristopher Triana; Mary
SanGiovanni; and my sons and daughter.

CONTENTS

WHAT DOESN'T DIE

INTRODUCTION

Welcome back to the world of *The Rising* – the (currently) seventh such book to take place in that setting. (The others being *The Rising, City of the Dead, The Rising: Selected Scenes From the End of the World, The Rising: Deliverance, Clickers vs. Zombies*, and *The Seven*). More on those, and this book, in a moment.

The title for this Introduction is also the title to one of my favorite later-stage Anthrax songs. I thought that was appropriate, given both my love of Anthrax's music, and the fact that drummer Charlie Benante provided this book's spectacular interior artwork. I'd also like to call attention to Wes Benscoter's cover for this book, which will no doubt bring to mind (for long-time readers) the classic cover to the first paperback edition of *The Rising* published by Leisure Books back in 2004. (It also has a cool Blue Oyster Cult album cover vibe, which I dig, since they are another of my favorite bands).

I've written elsewhere and mentioned in interviews about how much inspiration I drew from the Splatter-

punks when I was a young man. And it's true. I did. David
J. Schow, Joe R. Lansdale, Skipp & Spector, and their
extreme horror counterparts like Jack Ketchum and
Richard Laymon were northern stars on my literary
compass. But the guys from Anthrax were a constant influ-
ence on me as well. The public knows I'm eclectic as hell
when it comes to the types of music I listen to while I write
– everything from metal and hip-hop to Delta blues and
1970s honky-tonk country. But no band has fueled more of
my creations than Anthrax. Seriously, I did the math.
Prince, Bruce Springsteen, Ozzy, Iron Maiden, Motorhead,
Ice-T, Dr. Dre, Eminem, Johnny Cash, and Waylon
Jennings have all played a role, for sure, but at least once
in the creation of every book I've ever written and every
short story I've ever banged out, there's been something
by Anthrax playing in the background at some point.

Asking me for my favorite album by them is like
asking me which of my sons is my favorite, but since I
have two sons, I'll name two albums – *Among the Living*
and *Sound of White Noise*. When I was nineteen, I got in
trouble in the U.S. Navy for wearing a black *I'm The Man* t-
shirt underneath my uniform. One of the first short stories
I ever sold for publication was titled "Caught In A Mosh."
Hell, for the first seven or so years of my career, my
publicity photo – the one that goes in the back of the book
and that publicists send to the press and the stores – was
me in my black Anthrax hoodie. So yeah, I'm pretty
fucking psyched to have Charlie's artwork gracing the
cover of this collection. Thanks, man.

But I digress.

You cannot kill what doesn't die. And never has that
been truer than when it comes to *The Rising* franchise.

Shortly after *City of the Dead* was published back in 2005, I remember telling George Romero that I was done writing about the Siqqusim. "You say that now," he cautioned, "but you'll be surprised." And he was right, of course, as he was about most things (except for his loathing of fast zombies). No matter how hard I try to stay away, sooner or later my muse always brings me back to this place. In the twenty-five years that I've been doing this for a living, I've written and published well over fifty books and over three hundred short stories, plus comic books, graphic novels, a few audio serials, and other odds and ends. Of all my literary creations, it is this setting – the world of *The Rising* – that I have returned to the most.

One of those returns was the short story collection *The Rising: Selected Scenes From the End of the World*, in which I gave my fans and readers an opportunity to star in their own handcrafted short stories. They were the characters, and the details they provided me with about themselves were what informed the individual stories. The book was, and remains, a big hit with readers, but I had no plans to write a follow-up volume.

Until Bear got sick.

Bear is the longtime canine companion of author Kristopher Triana, and she's not just a good dog – she's one of the absolute best dogs I've ever had the pleasure of knowing. She travels with Kris to book signings and conventions and parties. Everyone who meets Bear falls in love with her.

In mid-2021, Bear was diagnosed with cancer. Kristopher was devastated, and all of us were heartbroken. But we found out that treatment could not only extend the remainder of her life, but remarkably improve the quality of her final days as well. Unfortunately, such treatment was prohibitively expensive, particularly on the salary of a full-time horror writer such as Kris. Still, he vowed to have that extra time with his friend, and he started a fundraiser – selling autographed books to fans, with the proceeds going toward Bear's treatment. Then other authors donated some autographed books of their own. And then, like I said a few paragraphs above, my muse returned to the world of *The Rising*, and I called Kristopher up and suggested we offer a bunch of brand-new short stories that take place in that setting. Each story would star the person who purchased it, and all of the funds would go to Bear's treatment. We made the reservations available and sold out fast. And then I contacted each of the people who'd bought one, and got them to tell me about themselves and where they live. And all of that material then got turned into zombie stories.

All of those stories are collected here, but there is also one other tale that was written long ago, way before Bear got sick. Indeed, that story – the first story in this book – predates even *The Rising*. You see, I began working on *The Rising* in 1998, but it wasn't published in hardcover until 2003 and in paperback (as I noted above) in 2004. For several years in between, I thought I'd never sell it so I cannibalized the novel twice for short story material. The first time was for a story called "Wild Kingdom," that I cowrote with Geoff Cooper. That was a retelling of Frankie's adventures at the zoo, with Coop adding his own spin. That story was published in the long out-of-print *4X4* *and* hasn't appeared since, other than on my Patreon. The second cannibalization was the first story you are about to read – a retelling of the first appearance of Ob. Like "Wild Kingdom," this story has long been out of print. Most of you have never seen it. I'm including it here as a special little bonus, even though it does not fit the parameters of the other stories herein.

Getting back to the other stories in this book, given the origins of this project, I was particularly delighted that many of the people who commissioned a tale asked me if I could include their own pets. Indeed, in one of the stories you are about to read, it is the pet who is the main protagonist. I like to think that one is probably Bear's favorite.

As I write this, I just saw Bear a month ago. Her life has been remarkably improved and extended. Like she does every time she sees me, she wagged her tail hard, and I got down on the floor with her and we gave each other big hugs and rolled around roughhousing together. And I thought about the folks who'd made that possible – the people in this book.

Let me introduce you to those people now. But be warned – there's other things lurking in these pages as well. If this is your first exposure to the world of *The Rising*, well… all you need to know is that everything that dies comes back to life. Not just people, but animals and insects and even plants. And they don't come back as mindless, slow-shuffling zombies. They are quick, cunning, and absolutely abhorrent – corpses inhabited but a collective group of supernatural entities known as the Siqqusim, whose only goal is to eradicate all life in cruel and sadistic fashion. Worse yet, they retain all of their host body's memories and abilities. So, if your partner was a special forces operative, and they died, now they're back as a demonically-possessed special forces operative. Even if you're lucky enough to destroy that corpse, the thing inside it will just move on to the next dead body and come after you again.

Because you cannot kill what doesn't die.

Enjoy! And on behalf of Bear and Kristopher Triana, thank you for your support.

Brian Keene
   Somewhere along the Susquehanna River
   April 2023

WAITING FOR INFINITY

HELLERTOWN, Pennsylvania

Mount Rushmore was speaking in tongues.

That was the first thing Baker noticed. The second thing was the baleful red glare coming from the granite eyes. It seemed to be pulling the chopper towards the living rock.

Struggling with the controls, Baker screamed as the founding fathers whispered obscenities in a multitude of languages.

The voice continued when he jerked awake, blearily raising his head from the desk. Saliva had pooled on his blotter, pulling at his skin as he sat up.

The blasphemies came from down the hall.

From the thing in Observation Room Number Six.

Baker blinked, unsure of what was happening. He always experienced a moment of confusion after a dream. He glanced around, letting the familiar settings settle into reality.

He was in his office, half a mile beneath Havenbrook. Above him, the gates of Hell had been opened wide. He had helped turn the key.

The room bore a resemblance to Southern Lebanon, the cumulative effects of three months without janitorial service. Dingy ceramic mugs, encrusted at the bottom with the fossilized remains of freeze-dried coffee. Papers, books, and diagrams lay strewn haphazardly about the room. The trashcan had long since overflowed. Its contents now spewed onto the floor. In the far corner, a dark stain marked where the fish tank had drained onto the carpet.

He shuddered.

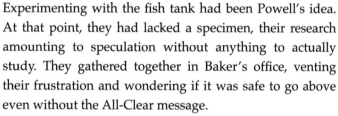

Experimenting with the fish tank had been Powell's idea. At that point, they had lacked a specimen, their research amounting to speculation without anything to actually study. They gathered together in Baker's office, venting their frustration and wondering if it was safe to go above even without the All-Clear message.

Powell had suggested, jokingly at first, that they try it out on one of Baker's prized tropical pets. Laughter and derision quickly turned to scientific seriousness when Baker agreed.

They netted one of the brightly colored fish, watching with cool detachment as it flopped and gulped in the smothering oxygen. Baker held it in his palm until it stopped quivering. Then they placed it back in the tank, where it floated on top of the briny water just as a dead fish was supposed to do.

Its behavior after death was surprisingly normal.

Disappointed, they had turned their attention back to the charts, heatedly arguing the evaporation rate of atomic nuclei.

It wasn't until two hours later, after the other scientists had retired to the common room for their tenth viewing of old *Jeopardy* episodes on video, that the fish started swimming again.

Baker was only dimly aware of the splashing at first; his attention focused on the game of solitaire laid out before him on the desk.

When the splashing became more violent and the tank actually shook on its stand, he looked up.

The water had already begun to turn red, tiny clouds of blood swirling amidst the brightly colored pebbles and plastic castle, as the dead fish began to hunt and kill its living brethren with a deliberate sort of glee.

At first, Baker gaped in horrified amazement. Then, gathering his wits, he dashed down the empty corridor and burst into the common room, gasping for breath, and summoning the others.

The slaughter was over by the time they crowded into the office. In the space of a few minutes, the fish had killed off every living thing in the tank. Innards and scales floated amidst the carnage.

"My God," gasped Harding.

"God," Baker spat. "*God* had nothing to do with *this*!"

"Baker…"

He thrust a finger at the tank. "This was mankind, Stephen. This was us!"

Harding stared at him, mouth working noiselessly, just as the fish had done. Powell, who had not adapted well to the crisis, was crying.

The fish finally noticed them. It stopped swimming and froze, staring at them with clear contempt.

Baker found himself drawn in fascination to the intelligence in that glare.

"Look at that," he whispered loudly. "It's studying us, just as we study it."

"What have we done," sobbed Powell. "Jesus fucking Christ, what have we done?"

"Powell," Harding snapped. "Get a grip on yourself, man. We need to learn as much as we can from this if we expect to undo…"

His reprimand was cut short by another splash. The fish thrashed around, stirring up the muck on the bottom of the tank, obscuring their view. It disappeared into the rear, hidden by a swirling cloud of blood and feces and slime.

"Somebody get the camcorder," Baker ordered. "We need to be documenting this."

Before they could, the entire tank stand moved. Water spilled over the top, running down the sides in crimson rivulets.

The fish retreated and then burst forth again, slamming itself into the front of the tank. Again and again, it charged the glass, heedless of the damage it was doing to itself. All the while, Baker could see the calculating malevolence that filled its dead eyes.

A network of cracks spread through the thick glass, spider-webbing up the sides. Just as Powell started to scream, the stand toppled over, crashing to the floor. Glass exploded, showering them all in glittering shards and brackish water.

The fish flopped onto the carpet and then, inexplicably, began to wriggle towards them. Shoving his books aside,

Baker leaped onto the desk while Harding retreated into the hall. Powell collapsed, shrieking and clawing at the walls while the thing closed the gap between them.

Above the scientist's terrified cries, Baker heard the noises it was making as it neared Powell's outstretched legs.

The fish was talking. He couldn't understand what was said, but the patterns were definitely that of intelligent speech.

With a sudden burst of strength, the thing shot forth towards Powell's groin. Powell screamed as the corrupted flesh brushed against his khakis, the mouth puckering.

Then Baker leaped to the floor, slamming the computer monitor down on it. Blow after repeated blow, he smashed the creature until there was nothing left but a viscous smear. He had been unaware that he was yelling until he felt Harding's hand on his shoulder.

The two men looked at each other, the enormity of what they had unleashed bearing down on them.

That night, Powell had sawn through his wrists with a butter knife from the cafeteria. They'd found him minutes later when they stopped in to administer a sedative.

He began moving soon after.

⸺

Baker looked away from the stain on the rug and closed his eyes. Slowly, he ran a hand through his graying hair and wept.

Down the hall, the thing in Observation Room Six continued ranting.

He fumbled in the congested ashtray, finding a partially smoked cigarette. Still weeping, he brought his lighter up to the ragged butt and thumbed it.

Nothing. No flame. Not even a spark. And the nearest lighter fluid was a half-mile above him in a world belonging to the dead.

He threw the useless lighter across the room. It struck a glass frame hanging on the wall. The newspaper that had been proudly displayed inside fluttered to the floor.

Wearily, Baker walked over and brushed away the broken glass. He began to laugh. The article was dated from earlier in the year.

BIG BANG MACHINE LEADS TO CONTROVERSY
By Monica Knight / Associated Press

A nuclear accelerator that was designed to replicate the Big Bang has drawn protests from a group of international physicists because of fears that it might cause "perturbations of the universe" that could harm the Earth. Indeed, one theory even suggests that it could form a black hole or "rend the fabric of space and time."

Havenbrook National Laboratories (HNL), one of the American government's foremost research bodies, has spent ten years building its $450 million Relativistic Heavy Ion Collider (RHIC) in Hellertown, Pennsylvania, a rural area near the New Jersey state border. A successful test firing was held this Friday and the first nuclear collisions are expected to take place within *the month, building up to full power around the beginning of autumn.*

Last week however, Stephen Harding, Havenbrook's director, set up a committee of physicists to investigate whether the project could go disastrously wrong. Harding was prompted by warnings from other physicists that there was a small but real risk that the machine had the power to create "strangelets," a new type of matter composed of sub-atomic particles called "strange quarks."

The committee is to examine the possibility that, once formed, strangelets might start an uncontrollable chain reaction that could convert anything they touched into more strange matter. The committee will also consider the less likely alternative that the colliding particles could achieve such a high density that they would form a mini black hole. In space, black holes generate intense gravitational fields that suck in all surrounding matter. The creation of one on Earth would be disastrous. The high density formed by the colliding particles could also, in theory, break down the barrier between our dimensions and others.

Professor Weston Whitman, director of the Center for Theoretical Physics at the Massachusetts Institute of Technology, who is on the committee, said he believed the risk was miniscule. "There have been fears that strange matter could alter the structure of anything nearby. The risk is exceedingly small."

• • •

Inside the collider, atoms of gold will be stripped of their outer electrons and pumped into one of two 2.4-mile circular tubes where powerful magnets will accelerate them to 99.9% of the speed of light.

The ions in the two tubes will travel in opposite directions to increase the power of the collisions. When they collide, they will generateminuscule fireballs of super-dense matter. Under these conditions, atomic nuclei evaporate into a plasma of even smaller particles called quarks and gluons. This plasma would then emit a shower of other particles as it cooled down.

Among the particles that would appear during this cooling are strange quarks. These have been detected in other accelerators but have always been attached to other particles. The RHIC, the most powerful machine yet built, has the ability to create solitary strange quarks for the first time since the universe began.

HNL officials confirmed that there had been discussions concerning the possibility of "perturbations in the universe." Timothy Powell, associate director of the RHIC, said that the committee would hold its first meeting shortly.

William Baker, professor of nuclear physics at Birmingham University, who is leading the scientific team for the RHIC, said that the chances of an accident were infinitesimally small, but that Havenbrook had a responsibility to assess them before proceeding. "The big question, of course, is whether our planet would vanish in the blink of an eye or perhaps the possibility of rending the fabric of space and time. It is astonishingly unlikely that there is any risk. We are not seeking to 'rip holes into other dimensions' as you put it. We are seeking to understand more about the universe and our place in it. The risk is so minuscule as to not even be considered."

Baker crumbled the paper in his fists, tearing it to shreds as his chest tightened.

The pain was extraordinary. Calm and detached from himself, he examined it in the same manner he had everything else in his life. His arms and face tingled as if they had fallen asleep.

His vision began to blur around the edges. *Tunnel vision*, he thought. *Perhaps this is why so many near death experiences report a tunnel.*

Down the corridor, in a soundproof room reinforced with six inches of steel and concrete, the thing that had once been Timothy Powell shouted in hungry gibberish. The meaningless words echoed through the empty underground complex, drifting up to the dead world above them.

Dying, Baker listened, wondering how long it would take before he returned.

SOPHIE'S FINAL CHOICE

SEDRO WOOLLEY, Washington

As she did every time she farted in her sleep, Sophie startled herself awake. She whipped her head from side to side, surprised to discover that it was daylight outside. Then she coughed – something that happened whenever she laid down for too long, a complication from her allergies. Sophie glanced around, verifying that her stuffed Hamburger, her Frankenstein's monster toy, and her Jack-Jack Incredibles toy from McDonalds were still where she'd put them before falling asleep. She panted with relief when she saw that they were. It was a small bit of normalcy and routine in an existence that had abandoned both.

Corey was where she'd left him before falling asleep as well.

He lay on the floor next to the couch, one arm flung over his forehead. His breathing was labored and shallow, and his skin was shiny and lathered in sweat. His eyes darted behind their closed lids. Whining, Sophie crossed the room, little Chihuahua nails clicking on the floor, and sniffed him. He smelled bad. The infection was worse today. She knew that smell all too well because that same sick stench had come from her at one point, in the past.

Corey had rescued Sophie from an abusive home about six years ago. She didn't remember much from her time before that – just confusing, jarring, shadowed images, glimpsed mostly in nightmares. But she remembered coming home to her new family, after Animal Control gave her to Corey. She remembered how he had to bathe her twice a day just to wash all of the pus and scabs from her hairless frame. She remembered how the infection was so bad that her outer layers of skin would slough off if anyone petted her too hard. It had taken months for Sophie to heal, and the stench that had wafted from her pores during that time was the same thing that oozed from Corey's now. Usually, because of her allergies, Sophie had to sniff really hard just to smell anything. But she didn't have to do that now.

He was still there, inside his body. He wasn't like those things outside. Those things that looked like humans and dogs and cats and birds…but weren't. Those dead things. In Sophie's experience, meat wasn't supposed to get up and walk around after it was dead. Dead meat was for eating, not walking. But all that had changed a month and a half ago. Now, instead of getting eaten, the meat did the eating.

Corey wasn't one of those things. Not yet. But unless he got better, he would be soon.

Sophie nosed Corey and whined, but he didn't respond. Then she tried licking his face. When that got no reaction, she ran and got her toy Hamburger, and brought it back to him. She dropped it on his chest and then lay down beside him. She crossed her paws and lowered her head, but she did not fall asleep. Instead, she waited dutifully, ignoring the pangs of hunger in her stomach.

Two months ago, Sophie had weighed almost seven pounds. Now, she weighed considerably less. She couldn't remember the last time she'd eaten, but it was definitely before Corey had gotten sick. She still had access to water. The toilet lid was up. But she was hungry. When she thought of ham or pizza, Sophie drooled. She'd found the last package of Marrosnacks — her favorite little milk bone nuggets — in the trash, but it had been empty. That hadn't stopped her from licking the crumbs from the container.

Corey groaned. The sound was weak. He did not gain consciousness. Sophie nervously chewed on her rear left leg in response.

Suddenly, there was a flash of movement from outside. She leaped up and darted for the window. Sophie never bothered to bark at squirrels or bugs or cats or other dogs because, quite frankly, they weren't worth her time, but she did bark at leaves. Leaves were her nemesis. But it wasn't a leaf scooting across the yard. It was one of those meat things. It had been a skunk when it was alive. Now, it was a shell, inhabited by something she didn't dare bark at because she didn't want to attract attention. The thing was missing its entire backend. Where its rear legs and tail should be, there was only desiccated flesh and shriveled entrails. She watched the creature crawl out of sight, and then turned her attention back to Corey.

Sophie liked wearing outfits, and he liked dressing her up in them. Maybe an outfit would help him feel better. She trotted over to the door, where her little yellow and black raincoat lay next to her unused leash. It had taken

Sophie a full day to work up the courage to relieve herself in the house, because that was a big no-no. But eventually, she hadn't been able to hold it. She never thought she'd miss the leash, but she did now.

Grabbing the raincoat in her teeth, she dragged it over to Corey and placed it next to him.

He opened his eyes, looked at her, and smiled.

Excited, Sophie stood on her back legs and waved her front paws, making an X gesture. She dropped back down on all fours, and her tail wagged furiously as she licked his face and nosed him.

Corey gave her a kiss, drew in a breath, and then slowly let it out.

He did not breathe again.

Sophie let out a mournful howl. She licked her mouth nervously and gnawed at her rear left leg again. And then she snorted.

Her stomach growled.

Corey was gone.

All that was left was meat.

Soon, something else would be inside of Corey, and that meat would rise again.

Sofie crept forward and sniffed him. She let out another mournful whine.

Then, she took a bite.

BODY TALK

J (Jason to his parents, and J to his friends — but never Jay, which was a full name) stared out over the balcony and watched the horde of corpses, studying them for behavioral clues. J had always been very observant and big on communication — particularly non-verbal cues and body language. Give him enough time to study someone, and he could tell you everything about them just from body talk.

But he couldn't determine anything about the dead, and that frustrated him.

J and Megan lived in a small, two-bedroom, top floor condominium. They had been in the process of buying a single-family home but then the world had gone to shit. Now, there would be no taking possession of the keys and no moving day. There would be no first holiday season spent in the new house. This was home — this three-story Briggs Chaney tomb.

J had always thought of the balcony as box seats. It was

perfectly positioned to allow him and Megan to look out onto the main road leading into their community. When the streets were active, it made for great people watching. Now, it served as a vantage point to watch the dead — more and more of which were steadily arriving. He caught a glimpse of his Toyota Camry below. Normally, he parked it in the lot behind the building, but he'd left it there instead for easier access should they need it. The light blue paint was covered in dirt and dried blood. He assumed that the latter must have come from the crowd of corpses shuffling around between the cars, all converging on the building. And not just dead people. Mixed among the rotting array were dead dogs and cats, a dozen or so squir-rels, something that was either a possum or a raccoon (it was hard to tell due to the extreme putrefaction), and even a dead deer. Luckily, there were no birds. At least, not yet. Or if there were, they were up on the roof above him, sitting where he couldn't see them.

And where they couldn't see him.

There were three other units on the top floor. The first had been occupied by a couple that J and Megan hadn't known, and had never gotten to know, because five days into the end of the world, the couple had died by mutual suicide — each swallowing a bottle of pills and then laying down beside each other in bed. J knew this because he'd found their suicide note while searching their apartment for food a few weeks later. Of course, they hadn't stayed dead long. No, like the rest of the mobile corpses, they'd reanimated and gone on a killing spree, breaking into the condo directly beneath J and Megan and slaughtering the family who lived there. J had never been fond of the people who'd lived below them. It had often been hard to understand exactly what was happening down there, as there were daily loud thuds and banging, and it frequently sounded as if they were walking on the ceilings. But the sounds of them dying had been much worse. The screams. The gurgles. The wet explosions.

Their other neighbors — Sam from the front condo and Dell from the unit to their side — had sheltered in place with J and Megan, holing up inside their unit. They'd barricaded the doors and windows, and focused on staying quiet as the zombies had rampaged through the rest of the building. Eventually, the chaos had subsided and the four of them got on with the business of surviving. They rationed their food and water, venturing out only a few times to raid the other units. The condo definitely had some advantages for the zombie apocalypse. It was on high ground. There was only one door in or out, plus a locked main entry door for the third floor. The only other means of access was the balcony itself. Early in the siege, Megan had suggested they fashion a rope ladder to drop over the side of the balcony in case they needed to escape. J had vetoed this idea, pointing out that they didn't have any rope, and even if they had, climbing a rope ladder was far more difficult than it seemed in the movies. Now, as the stench of the crowd below wafted up to him, he saw just how futile such an attempt would have been. Descending from the balcony would be like dropping into a meat grinder or a swimming pool filled with ravenous piranha.

He heard a distant, steady banging noise. The zombies had reached the third floor.

The wind shifted, and a gust of cool air washed over the balcony, pushing the stench away. J shivered inside his Philadelphia Eagles zip-up hoodie. The seasons were changing. He no longer knew what day it was. He couldn't even be sure about the month. But it was easy to see that autumn was on the way, and winter would soon follow. J hated the cold.

He shoved his sticky hands inside the pockets of his gore-encrusted sweat pants and noticed that his sock game was off. There was blood splattered across the Marvel Comics characters stretched cross his ankle socks as well. He pulled his hands free and studied them. Blood had dried beneath his fingernails and caked in the webbing between his fingers.

J sighed. The banging sound continued, steady and determined. He was sure the barricade would hold a while longer, though.

He couldn't go back inside the condo because he didn't want to see Megan. She'd still been moving when he'd come out onto the balcony. She'd still been talking, too, and that was the worst part — the things her corpse said. He knew it wasn't her. It was something else, some sort of entity that had taken possession of her dead body the way a person drove a car. It used her mouth and voice, but it wasn't *her*.

There was so much he didn't know. So much he didn't understand about these things. And that frustrated him almost to despair.

It had been a snake. A simple little copperhead, one of the few venomous snakes in Maryland. J had never seen one in the wild and would have doubted they existed in a suburban area like Silver Spring, but the proof was undeniable. They had always slept in shifts — J and Megan standing watch during the day, and Sam and Dell doing the same at night. Somehow, the dead snake had gotten past all the barricades and barriers. J supposed it had probably slithered through the ductwork or a vent.

However it had gained access, the tiny creature — less than ten inches long and no thicker than his middle finger — had managed to undo everything they'd built, upending their survival in a matter of minutes. It bit Sam, pumping venom into him. J and Megan had awoken to his screams and found Dell kneeling over him on the floor, unsure of what to do as the venom began to take hold. They hadn't even realized the snake was still there until it bit Dell as well. Then, while J had destroyed the snake, smashing it into a red smear with the replica baseball bat of Negan from *The Walking Dead* that Megan had bought him, Sam died. Dell must have not realized it at first, judging by the shocked confusion in his expression as Sam sat up, bit into his throat, and ripped it out, spitting a wad of flesh onto the floor like it was phlegm.

J had always kept weapons hidden around the condo— bats, old workout bars, and even a retractable baton. As Sam shoved the gurgling Dell aside and focused on Megan, J had tossed her the Negan bat and then pulled out a knife. But Sam had been faster, even in death. He'd lunged for the bat and caught it in mid-air. Then he'd turned the weapon on Megan, breaking her arms and legs before J could reach her. He'd tackled the zombie from behind, sending them both crashing over the couch. Then, before Sam could react, J stabbed him in the head with the knife, grunting as he tried to push the blade through the skull. He barely heard Megan's scream over his own furious cries.

Eventually, Sam jittered and then went limp, as if someone had flipped off a switch. J clambered to his feet, realizing that Megan was no longer screaming.

Dell had already gotten to her.

He'd snatched up the bat and used it to smash Dell's

head in. Then he'd knelt over Megan, holding her as the light went out of her eyes — and watching as, a few moments later, something else looked out of them for the first time.

That was when he'd retreated out onto the balcony. He hadn't been back inside since. She wasn't able to get to him. Not with two broken arms and two equally broken legs. And yet, somehow, she'd managed to alert the other creatures to his presence.

"How?" he muttered.

There was so much he didn't know, and watching them was teaching him nothing. He needed to get closer.

J stood up and peered over the balcony railing. The creatures roared, shouting at him to jump. He considered it, but if he landed on his head, he wouldn't reanimate. Of that much he was certain. And if he was going to become one of them to better understand, then that was no good. The zombies jeered and yelled. One of them wore a dirty, tattered Redskins jersey. J gave it the finger.

Shaking his head, he stepped back. The pounding was louder now.

No. He would let Megan do it. She couldn't hold a knife, but she still had her teeth.

He would go back inside, lay down next to her, and talk one last time. When she'd had breast cancer, he had gotten her through the tough days — listening, guiding, and holding her. Maybe now, she could do the same for him.

Smiling, J opened the door.

PLAN D

RIVER CITY, Iowa

Alexander Bailey glanced again at the gas gauge and pondered Plan C.

His original plan had started out okay. He'd intended to reach his cousin Matt's house — a fifteen-minute drive when the dead weren't walking the streets. He'd packed all of the canned food and bottled water in his home, along with some changes of clothing, extra socks and boxer shorts, the large hunting knife he kept at the bottom drawer of his dresser, a few paperback books, a bottle of body wash, and a bottle of hand sanitizer, and loaded them all into his red Nissan Frontier. The vehicle had originally belonged to Alex's father, who'd been murdered when Alex was fourteen. Now it was his. He liked to think that in some way — the fact that the vehicle itself weighed heavily into his survival plan — his father was watching out for him.

Making sure the coast was clear, he'd gone back into

his home and grabbed his metal baseball bat and Buttercup. He'd had her since she was a kitten, a present from his mother — a grey striped beauty with a smattering of light calico colors and a left eye that was slightly crossed. Gone were the days when Buttercup had been able to fit into the palm of his hand, but she'd been his constant companion through two big changes of residence and two equally big relationships. Buttercup hated car rides, and as soon as Alex had her loaded into the Nissan, she'd begun to meow mournfully, hiding on the floor between the passenger's seat and the back seat.

"It's okay," he assured her. "Just play with Mr. Raccoon."

He reached for the squeaky toy raccoon and realized it was still inside the home.

And that was when Plan A fell apart.

Cursing, he'd hopped out of the Frontier and hurried back inside. He found Mr. Raccoon wedged under a chair and rushed back outside with him again...

...only to nearly collide with a zombie. He didn't recognize the corpse. Chuckling, it grasped at him, fingers clawing. Too late, he realized that he'd left the baseball bat in the Nissan. He'd squeezed Mr. Raccoon in his fist and punched the ghoul right in the nose. The toy squeaked from the impact. The zombie tottered backward, still laughing, as he dodged past it and ran to the vehicle, getting inside and locking the doors just as the creature reached them.

Panicked, Alex ran over the zombie and blew out one of his front tires in the process. The corpse caught on the vehicle's undercarriage, and he dragged it down the road, leaving a grisly smear in their wake. By the time he and Buttercup reached Matt's house, most of the tire had fallen away, leaving a bare rim.

Matt, who had served in the 82nd Airborne, suggested they take his car and go to the home of his friend Jerry, who was a Vietnam veteran and had a house full of guns — not all of which were legal. The four of them would then drive to Alex's mother's house. She lived with his stepfather about an hour and a half to the north on a piece of land out in the country that included a one-story farmhouse, a dilapidated barn, a long chicken coop, and a corn crib which had been converted into a workshop. Behind the house was a pasture with a small pond.

That had been Plan B, and it had fallen apart upon their arrival at Jerry's place when they discovered that Jerry was already dead, and his vast collection of armaments were now in the hands of his demonically possessed corpse. The thing that once had been Jerry shot Matt on the porch, and then shot up most of his car, as well. Alex and Buttercup had barely escaped, and by the time they raced away — with Alex now driving Matt's shot-up car — one glance in the rearview mirror showed Matt grabbing a gun from Jerry and joining in the melee. His reanimation had occurred that fast.

In addition to being riddled with bullet holes, upon reaching Matt's house again, the car was hemorrhaging oil and steam leaked from the radiator. Worse, the dead were roaming in and out of Matt's house, and canvassing the neighborhood looking for survivors. Alex had loaded himself, Buttercup, and Mr. Raccoon back into the Nissan, locked the doors, and tried to figure out what to do next.

That was when he'd come up with Plan C.

There was no way the Nissan would make it to his

mother's home, much less the other side of town. But it might make it as far as the River City Theater, where both Alex and Matt had worked before everything went to shit. The top four floors of the massive building would be too difficult to barricade, but the basement — where both he and Matt had offices — was protected by a big metal sliding door that was nearly impregnable. Several years before, when River City had flooded and the electricity was out, the theater's executive director — upon discovering that the electronic keypads for the door no longer worked — had tried to break it down with an axe. That barely made a dent in it. But Alex knew how to get it open, electricity or no. More importantly, he knew how to keep it shut. If he and Buttercup could make it into the basement without being seen, they could hole up safely there for as long as they needed. Hell, if they needed to, they could even retreat to the subbasement, which was accessible only via a small room beneath the stage.

So, he and Buttercup had coasted along in the Nissan, driving on the rim, until they reached the theater.

And that was when Plan C collapsed.

It turned out that Matt and Jerry had gotten there first. They, along with the corpses of several of Alex's coworkers and a smattering of complete strangers, were waiting when he and Buttercup arrived. As their weapons snapped up, he'd stomped the gas and sped away, shedding sparks on the road behind him.

Having no more plans, he'd simply fled town, pushing the Nissan to its absolute limits. The car shuddered and squealed. The transmission made an awful grinding sound. Sparks continued to trail them, spinning off from the rim. The gas gauge began to dip. And Buttercup had meowed incessantly until they reached the River City limits.

Alex had guided the lurching vehicle into a field full of tall grass, and then he'd killed the engine.

And that was where they were now.

"Okay, Buttercup," he whispered. "Plan D."

He crawled into the backseat with her and opened a can of cat food. While she licked and gorged, he opened a can of vegetables for himself. When they were both finished, he unscrewed the lid from a bottle of water, poured some in the empty can for Buttercup, and then drank the rest.

Ever since she was a kitten, Buttercup had always preferred to be in the same room as Alex. And now that they were no longer driving, she settled down and stopped meowing. Indeed, as she rubbed her face against his, Buttercup began to purr.

He leaned back in the seat. She climbed into his lap and cuddled. Alex glanced around the interior of his father's vehicle. He had duct tape underneath the seat. If he covered the windows and the windshield, and they were quiet, this might just work. Going to the bathroom might be a problem for them both, but he was sure they could figure something out.

Yes, given their other options, this seemed like the best plan.

Plan D.

Alex closed his eyes. Buttercup purred, kneading her paws against his thigh.

After a while, they both slept.

BUNKER HILL REVISITED

BUNKER HILL, Illinois

Life was such a wheel, Anthony Naylor remembered Stephen King writing, *that no man could stand upon it for long. And in the end, it always came around to the same place again.*

Or something like that. He couldn't be sure. The problem with his love of pop culture artifacts was that now, in this crisis situation, they all seemed to blend together into a brain-stew. *Vampirella* and *Swamp Thing* comics, episodes of *Supernatural* and *Buffy the Vampire Slayer*, and novels like *Soldier Boys* and *Harry Potter* all blended together. But he was pretty sure King had written that, or something close to that.

The wind shifted, and he smelled the dead again. Anthony decided there was another quote that fit their situation — the scene between Meatwad and Frylock in the *Aqua Teen Hunger Force* finale, when Meatwad asked Frylock if they would be on television forever, and Frylock answered yes before the screen made an abrupt smash cut to the production company logo. Just yesterday, Anthony's daughter had asked him if they would live here in the church steeple forever. And any minute now, the television screen showing their lives would probably smash cut to black.

He stared down at the dead, and then glanced back at his family. His wife, Haley was huddled with their daughter, Rylie, and their two small dogs, Odie and Boots. The latter was a Chihuahua Patterdale Terrier mix who never stopped licking unless asleep. But Boots wasn't licking now, because Boots was dead — bitten as they raced from the car into the church, and then dispatched by Anthony before Boots could rise again and do more than lick. He'd done the deed here, in the belfry. Odie had refused to leave Boot's side ever since.

Anthony had grown up in Bunker Hill. It was a small town, with vast stretches of rural countryside surrounding it, so when the dead began to outnumber the living and started going door to door in search of victims, Anthony had loaded the family into the car and fled their boarded-up basement in Pekin, driving two hours south to Bunker Hill, only to find out that the situation here hadn't been any better.

Before the Rising, the town's population had numbered below two thousand. Most of those residents were still here, and currently assembled below. Some of them were still whole. Others were in pieces. All of them were dead, including his mother, Lauri, his oldest brother Randy Junior, and his sister-in-law Sarah. Both his mother and his brother had called out to him, laughing and jeering, taunting him to come down. Sarah hadn't joined in because she no longer had a lower jaw. Anthony hadn't seen any sign of their one-year-old son, Clyde, and assumed the boy was *dead* dead, rather than the walking dead.

He thought that was probably for the best.

Anthony glanced back at Rylie, curled up against Haley, and blinked back tears.

His other brother Alex lived with his family in a small village a few miles west of town. Anthony second guessed himself now as he heard multiple sets of feet climbing the stairs. Maybe he should have tried to get to their house instead. Or maybe they should have never left home at all. Haley had been against it, wanting to stay near her own family instead. And Anthony had felt some misgivings about leaving his comic book collection and other things behind. But they'd had no idea if Haley's family were even alive, and things like movies and books didn't come before his own family's safety, and so he had insisted.

And now, here they were.

He would never turn thirty-one. Never visit Loch Ness. Never publish that short story he'd written back in high school. Never make love with Haley again. Never see the new *Resident Evil* movie. Never see Rylie head off for her first day of school, or her prom, or walk her down the aisle on her wedding day.

Anthony stared out over the rooftops as the zombies began to pound on the other side of the trapdoor. Bunker Hill was nothing like its namesake in Massachusetts. The town consisted of a Dollar General, a sandwich shop, and two gas stations. A high school and a primary school were the only sources of education. The rest of the buildings were houses and churches and bars. Two main roads intersected in the town square, which was an elevated hill topped with a flagpole and a statue of Abraham Lincoln.

The zombies had cut the head off the statue and strung body parts together on the pole.

He'd never been sure why the town's forefathers had named it Bunker Hill. Perhaps they'd been enamored of the original — that famous battle in the American Revolution, where one thousand, two hundred colonists — including over one hundred African Americans — had successfully repelled two onslaughts from British troops. The third assault had faltered only because the colonists had run out of ammunition.

A mistake that Anthony had made sure not to repeat.

He checked the Ruger nine-millimeter in his hand. There were three rounds left. One for each of his loved ones — but not enough for him.

Anthony believed in God. He read his Bible every day, but the Good Book had offered no solace or words of wisdom during the Rising.

He turned back to his family. Odie stared up at him with mournful eyes. Anthony knelt and smelled his wife's hair. He kissed her forehead.

"I love you," he whispered.

Nodding, she rasped, "I love you, too."

"Are the dead people going to get in?" Rylie asked. "Will they take me away from you?"

"No, baby," Anthony promised. "I'll make sure we stay together. Close your eyes now, and hug Mommy tight."

She did, and then Anthony kept his promise. The zombies fell quiet momentarily as the three shots rang out, echoing through the belfry and out over the town.

Anthony stood there, shoulders stooped, head low, eyes closed. He didn't want to look at them. Didn't want to see. Instead, he turned toward the trap door and let the gun slip from his hands. It clattered onto the floor.

His best friend Andrea had also lived in Bunker Hill. They hadn't spoken since the phones went down, but when he'd last heard from her, she had been alive.

"Hey," he yelled, his voice raw and hoarse with emotion. "You things listening to me?"

Several loathsome voices called out at once, affirming that they were.

Anthony asked for Andrea by name. There was a moment of silence, and then a single voice spoke.

"I'm here. We are all here. We are more than the stars! More than infinity."

It was Andrea's voice but also not her voice. Anthony had enough experience with the risen to know that it wasn't really her. Something else—some kind of demon— was inside his friend's corpse.

But he hoped it would still look like her.

He told them he was going to open the door and that he wanted Andrea to be the one to do it. And then he removed the barricade.

The zombies rushed in. Andrea was in the lead. She charged toward him, and they locked together in one last hug. As her teeth brushed against his throat, Anthony stepped backward, holding on to the embrace as they both toppled over the edge. He caught one glimpse of his family, and hoped to see them again in a moment as he and Andrea plummeted to the ground.

NEMBROTTO

ALBANY, NY

All things considered, Sabas Moreno didn't mind the end of the world so much. He was single, with no family left even before the event that people called the Rising, and he had no wife or children. He'd been able to count his friends on one hand, and indeed, if a zombie had bitten off one of his fingers, it wouldn't have impeded that final tally. When the dead began slaughtering the living, those few friends were quickly cut down, and were all gone now. When it came to day-to-day survival, he only had himself to worry about, and no one left to miss.

Except Hannibal.

Even now, Sabas could clearly remember the day Hannibal had come into his life. He'd been browsing at a bookstore and the girl he'd been dating at the time rushed in, gushing about the one-hundred percent purebred, tri-colored, Pembroke Welsh Corgi in the pet store next door. Sabas, who'd never had the desire for a pet, had accompanied her back to the store out of a sense of disinterested but resigned obligation. Upon first glance, the dog had looked like some canine Frankenstein's monster fashioned out of spare parts — the head of a German Shepard, the tiny legs of a Dachshund, the torso of a plump bulldog, and a stub rather than a tail. The thing looked ridiculous, and Sabas had scoffed. It wasn't until he found out that the animal shared a birthday with Joey Ramone that he decided to take it home.

And that was how he'd ended up with Hannibal.

The dog had been his constant companion for twelve and a half years, until cancer tore through him so quickly that Sabas never had time to even explore the various treatment options.

After that, Sabas's daily greasepaint – his mask that he used for the public and society – started to crack. He cared very little about keeping it on.

Sabas wasn't a sociopath or a psychopath. At least, he didn't think so. Any official diagnosis identifying him as such would have involved going to a therapist, and he felt about them the way he felt about everybody else. He was a self-diagnosed misanthrope. A loner who hated most people on most days. One of his exes had once described him as "not exactly suicidal, but wouldn't rush to get out of the way of an oncoming car." She wasn't wrong. Sabas wasn't afraid of death. He didn't exactly welcome it, but he didn't fear it if it came. He'd been facing death most of his life. As a young man, thanks to an autoimmune disor-der, he'd been given medicine to suppress his immune system. But the dosage had been too high, and it was supposed to have destroyed his liver and kidneys by now. That hadn't happened yet, even with the copious amounts of vodka he consumed. The way he saw it, Sabas was at

least fifteen years past his expiration date. Alive. Dead. He
didn't care. It would happen, eventually.

In the meantime, he just kept trucking, and tried to
have fun.

As he did every time he went outside the warehouse,
Sabas wondered if today would be when the fun stopped,
and death finally caught up with him. He checked his gear
– makeshift body armor that he'd fashioned from plastic
sheeting, an umpire's mask he'd looted from a sporting
goods store, and his two machetes, sheathed on each side
of his hips. He'd owned the latter since he was seventeen
years old. And as for the former? It was hard to find body
armor for somebody his size. He knew all too well what an
imposing figure he was – a large white guy covered in
tattoos who, throughout his life – including during his
arrests – was constantly asked if he was affiliated with a
motorcycle gang. Even now, with food supplies dwin-
dling, he hadn't lost any of that mass.

Sabas had worked in warehousing since he was nineteen years old – sometimes legitimately and other times
for various organized crime families. He'd started with
Marano Family associates Tony Genova and Vince Napoli.
Occasionally, a truckload of televisions would disappear
from the warehouse, or a pallet of air conditioning units
would vanish off the dock. Sabas always arranged for
these missing shipments to end up in Tony and Vince's
hands. From there, he'd worked his way up to doing other
things for them – and for other groups, as well, including
the Russians and the Greeks. It was one of those later illicit
activities for the Italians that had earned him the nickname
Nembrotto. The first few times Tony and Vince had called
him that, Sabas thought it must be Italian for "Hey you." It
wasn't until he read a side-by-side translation of

Alighieri's *Inferno* that Sabas found out it was instead Italian slang for the Hebrew word Nimrod, which meant 'great hunter.'

The warehouse he currently resided in had been one he'd worked in before the dead started coming back to life. It was outside of Albany, within spitting distance of the Hudson River and close to the mountains and forests. Sabas had moved here when things started to get bad and spent two full days fortifying and securing it. Until recently, it had been well-stocked, and while he still had plenty of water, food was beginning to run low. He would have to forage through nearby stores and homes within the next few days. Otherwise, the warehouse had everything he needed to survive. It was safe – much safer than hiding out inside a suburban house or apartment building. The only thing he didn't like about it was the silence. Sabas wasn't one to normally mind being alone, but the stillness of the place preyed on him in ways he hadn't anticipated, reminding him that he was the only living thing here. For some reason, it made him miss Hannibal even more. If the Corgi were still alive, he'd be his constant shadow, and a comfort at night, which was when that cloying silence seemed its worst.

"Getting maudlin," he grumbled, and then cleared his throat. It was sore from disuse. He paused, trying to remember the last time he'd spoken aloud. It had been several days, at least.

Sabas walked over to the warehouse door and listened. It seemed quiet outside. He frowned, slightly disappointed. He liked it when a small group of zombies clustered around the building's exterior. It was fun to suddenly burst from the door, machetes swinging, and carve them up. It was one thing to scare the living, but it was an even bigger thrill to get that same sort of reaction from the dead.

Moving with caution, he opened the door and slipped outside. The docks and the parking lot were deserted, save for the rotting remains of a few zombies he'd slain on previous excursions. As he crept across the pavement, dead leaves, broken glass, and an occasional bone crunched beneath his boots. Even out here, under the blue sky, he couldn't escape the stillness. There were no birds singing. No cars driving by. No tractor trailers idling. No people talking. The only sound was the wind blowing through some nearby trees.

He glanced up at the sun, trying to calculate how far across the sky it was and how much more daylight he had left. He considered making the hike into town to restock his food. Maybe he could fill up a shopping cart and wheel it back here.

He'd reached the wire fence at the far edge of the parking lot when the wind brought him a joyful new noise.

The bark of a dog.

Sabas grinned. Zombie animals could be a challenge. Often, depending on the condition of the corpse, they moved faster than their human counterparts. Maybe today would offer some fun, after all.

He hurried to open the security gate, fumbling with the chain lock. Then he rushed in the direction of the commotion. It was coming from a paved turnaround area next to a flat, desolate field of brown grass. He couldn't see the dog because there were several big trucks, long since abandoned by their owners, obstructing his view. As he rushed toward them, the barking grew louder. It was accompanied by fierce growls. Slowing his pace, Sabas drew both machetes and stalked forward, trying to remain stealthy.

He drew alongside one of the trailers, and heard voices. The dog wasn't alone. He dropped to his hands and knees and peered beneath the truck. He saw four dog legs, and six pairs of human legs. Frowning, he flattened himself onto his belly and then crawled under the trailer, snaking closer to the commotion.

The dog was a mixed-breed male. It contained notable traces of Beagle and some black and tan coonhound, but there were other breeds in its genetic makeup, as well – a true mutt. It was bigger than Hannibal had been, but not by much. Most amazingly, it was alive. But the three zombies that had encircled it seemed intent on not allowing that for much longer. The dog circled and pranced, haunches raised, baring its teeth and growling again. Laughing and jeering, the zombie feigned lunges at it. Sabas saw that none of them were armed.

Gritting his teeth, he pulled himself halfway out from under the trailer, far enough that he could lift his arms. Then he raised both of the machetes and swung, hacking the closest corpse's feet off at the ankles. The blades vibrated as they struck bone, and he felt the jolt go through both of his arms. Even as the dead man toppled over, Sabas scrambled to his feet. The zombie, heedless of its missing feet, rolled over and crawled toward him, muttering curses.

"Fucking meat," it grumbled. "I'm going to stick those things up your ass."

Sabas didn't waste breath with a response. Instead, he simply swung again, cleaving one of the blades through the creature's skull, destroying the brain. The zombie immediately went limp. Its companions forgot about their prey and turned toward him. Sabas assumed the dog would take advantage of the distraction and run away, but instead, it leaped into the air and ripped out one of their throats. The dead man's head lolled backward. Sabas finished the job, lopping it off. Then he turned his attention to the third zombie. The creature lunged, arms outstretched, but Sabas ducked down and hacked at its knees. Then he sprang to his feet again and raised the machete to deliver another blow. The dog darted back into the fray and seized one of the monster's hands in its teeth.

"Drop it," Sabas said. "Do you know drop it?"

The dog was indeed familiar with the command. He let go of their opponent's hand and retreated to a safe distance. Then he sat down on his back legs and cocked his head quizzically.

Sabas grinned. "Good boy."

Then he cut the zombie's head off. It fell to the ground and rolled over on one side. The creature's mouth moved, trying to speak. The eyes glared at him. Sabas kicked it across the lot.

Sabas and the dog stood looking at each other while the dead man's headless corpse bled out between them.

"Good boy," he repeated.

The dog wagged its tail and took a cautious step toward him.

Sabas wiped his machetes on the zombie's pants and then sheathed them. He knelt and held out one hand. "Come on. Come here. It's okay."

The dog licked its lips and then edged closer. It stretched out its nose, sniffed his fingers, and then gave a joyous bark. Laughing, Sabas petted its neck and back. The dog's tail whipped back and forth.

"Want to come stay with me?"

The dog barked again.

"Okay. Come on."

He started back toward the warehouse, and the dog trotted along at his side, panting and sniffing.

"Tomorrow we'll have to go hunt up some more food," Sabas told the dog. "And I guess we'll need to give you a name, too. I don't see a collar on you."

The dog glanced up at him, wagged its tail again, and then went back to sniffing the ground.

"You're a tracker," Sabas observed. Already his throat, which had been sore earlier, felt better from talking. "How about I call you Nembrotto?"

Nembrotto barked, and the two of them went home.

INTO THE FIRE

ALBUQUERQUE, New Mexico

They were just a few miles west of West of Westland on Interstate 40 when the truck ran out of gas. Benjamin Baca had known it was going to happen, but there wasn't much he could do about it, and he hadn't wanted to alarm his family. They were already in a perpetual state of shock, given the events of the last month — or months, perhaps? He could no longer tell. The passage of time, the act of marking squares off a calendar, the concept of naming the days of the week — all of those had fallen by the wayside. Regardless, his family were all suffering from post-traumatic stress disorder. Or maybe just traumatic stress disorder, since post would indicate the past, and they were still living and surviving in the now. To tell the truth, he was probably suffering from it, as well. How could he not be? How could anyone not be?

As the engine sputtered and died, he turned to them. His wife, Crystal. His thirteen-year-old son, Benjamin

Junior. And their two-year-old daughter, Emma. All crammed into the cab with him. A cab that was already hot and stifling, and would soon turn into an oven.

That was the problem with the zombie apocalypse happening in Albuquerque. It was a desert, which meant blisteringly hot temperatures in the summer. Everything that died — be it human or animal — came back as the living dead. And started to rot in the heat. And while the cunning cruelty and sheer evil of the undead was astonishing, it was their combined stench that was truly overwhelming. Their numbers grew with each passing day, and with each living thing that they killed, the stench grew stronger, seeming to hang over the region like a thunderstorm.

Sitting on her brother's lap, Emma hadn't noticed their predicament. Her attention was absorbed by the game she was playing on her brother's tablet. Benjamin idly wondered how they would recharge the device once the battery ran low. But while she was oblivious, Crystal and Benjamin Junior weren't. They stared at him, eyes wide.

He forced a smile that felt more like a grimace, and said, "Don't worry."

"It will be okay," his son replied.

Crystal didn't speak, but she reached out and patted his leg.

Taking a deep breath, Benjamin squinted against the glare of the sun and stared out at the landscape. He spotted two abandoned cars, a wrecked tanker truck, and a Love's Truck Stop. And miles and miles of desert. Curiously, there were no zombies. At least, not that he could see. A small flock of seven or eight birds circled overhead, but they were too high up to tell if they were dead or alive.

He exhaled. "Okay."

"What's the plan?" Crystal asked.

"Head for the truck stop."

She visibly stiffened.

His son frowned. "But what if those things are inside?"

"They might be," Benjamin admitted, "but we can't stay here inside the truck. We'll cook to death."

"I'd rather cook than get eaten," his son replied.

"You say that now, but give it a few hours. And nobody is going to get eaten. We've stayed alive this long, right?"

Emma began to stir, realizing that they were no longer driving.

"I'll go first," Benjamin said. "Scout around, and make sure it's clear. You guys stay here and keep the doors shut."

His son stirred. "I'm going with you."

"No, you're not."

Before they could debate it any further, Benjamin grabbed his AK-47 from behind the seat, noticing as he did that the bayonet lug was loose. He tightened it as best he could with his fingers, and then reached under the seat and pulled out a handgun. He offered it to Crystal.

"The Makarov?" She accepted the weapon. "But won't you need it?"

"I've got this."

"But the Makarov is your favorite."

"And there's a reason for that. Same reason I'm leaving it with you."

He took another deep breath.

"Be careful," Crystal whispered.

Nodding, he exhaled and quietly opened the door.

The heat slammed into him like a physical force. He stepped down out of the cab and felt the temperature through the soles of his shoes, radiating up from the highway's surface. Closing the door behind him, Benjamin crept forward, eyes darting back and forth for any sign of movement. He was relieved to see the birds fly on, heading south.

Little early for them to be going south for the winter, he thought. He wondered again how much time had passed and where they were on the seasonal calendar. Winter would be a welcome change right now, not only giving them a respite from the noxious air, but from the heat, as well.

He blamed himself for their current situation, even though there hadn't been much else they could have done. Having served eight years as an infantry medic in the New Mexico Army National Guard (including a tour of duty in Kosovo), Benjamin had always been conscience about preparedness. When the Rising had begun, he'd figured his family would be safe until things returned to normal. They had plenty of food and fresh water, and a small armory in their house. He collected military surplus rifles, and in addition to the AK-47 and the Makarov, they'd owned an AR-15, a Chinese SKS, a couple of Mausers, a Mosins Nagant, a beautiful Lee Enfield, and an M1 Garand, as well as several other handguns. His first instinct had been to bug out to a less-densely populated area, like the nearby Sandia Mountains. But things happened quickly, and it soon became apparent that sheltering in place was the better option. As a result, Benjamin had done his best to arm the neighborhood, and had given out most of his weapons to his friends and neighbors. The problem with that was that once they died, those friends and neighbors came back as heavily armed zombies, shooting at him with his own guns.

Eventually, when their situation had become untenable, they'd fled the house, hopped into the truck he drove for work, and hit the road. Benjamin had heard from a ham radio operator that there was a huge explosion at Kirtland Air Force Base, and the area around it was covered in some kind of toxic dust, so they'd headed west instead of east.

And now here they were — out of gas in the middle of the desert.

Out of the frying pan and into the fire.

He caught movement out of the corner of his eye, and instinctively swiveled the rifle toward it. A dead rattlesnake wriggled toward him. He knew it was dead because its back half was missing. The creature trailed entrails through the dirt as it slithered onto the road. Grimacing, Benjamin waited until it was closer, and then — not wanting to attract attention with a gunshot — rammed the bayonet through its head. The snake stopped moving and died again.

He glanced up, intent on flashing his family a thumbs up, and saw a second zombie shuffling toward the truck. Like the snake, its loathsome state was all-too apparent. One of the creature's arms was missing, and one of its eyeballs hung from a strand of gristle, where it had shriveled up and dried against the corpse's cheek. A chunk of its scalp was missing, as was a fragment of the skull beneath it, and the thing's brains were exposed. Benjamin shuddered as he watched flies buzz in and out of the festering wound.

"Hi," the monster slurred, its tone almost congenial. It raised a hand and waved. *"Nice to see you. Haven't seen any other living things around here for several days. Or any more of our kind, either. It's just been me and him."*

Despite all of his training, Benjamin hesitated. Of all the reactions he'd expected from the creature, this was not one he had anticipated. He snapped the rifle up, set the stock against his shoulder and armpit, and took aim at the zombie's center mass. Then, he corrected himself and sighted on its head instead.

"*No need for that,*" the corpse said. "*I'll be leaving soon. Our time here is over. Heading on to the next level. Now, the Elilum will get a turn.*"

Benjamin licked his parched lips. "The..."

"*Elilum. See these flies buzzing in and out of my host's head? Everything we did to your kind, the Elilum will do to them and all of the other lesser lifeforms. Then...when they're finished, the Teraphim will arrive and burn this planet to a cinder. You think it's hot now? Try to stay alive until then, and you'll really see how hot it can get. I envy you that. I haven't watched them work since...well, I guess it must be one million of your years or so. We spent all of that time in the Void and now that we're free it's just work, work, work. Never a momen—*"

Benjamin charged, again not wanting to attract attention with a rifle shot. The zombie's expression was one of surprise. It flailed at him with its one remaining arm, but he sidestepped the blow and buried the bayonet in the creature's exposed brains, stirring them around until they bubbled out of the cavity like cottage cheese.

He stood over the corpse for a long time, panting. When he looked up, his son was sliding toward the driver's side door. Benjamin motioned at him to stay inside the vehicle, and then headed toward the truck stop. He spent ten minutes sweeping the entire structure and all of the surrounding area and found it clear. Finished, he stood outside by a row of gas pumps. Dead cockroaches crunched beneath his feet.

The zombie had been telling the truth.

As he walked back outside and motioned at his family that it was safe to approach, Benjamin wondered what else it had been telling the truth about. As Crystal and the kids hurried toward him, Benjamin looked west, into the setting sun. He wiped the sweat from his brow and thought again about how hot it was.

He felt something brush against his leg, beneath his pants. Startled, he glanced down and saw that the dead cockroaches had begun to move again.

WASTED TIME

Kennewick, Washington

The sky over Coyote Bob's Roadhouse Casino was a peaceful shade of blue, the clouds shot through with hues of red as the sun continued its ascent over a dead world. Andy Martin stood on the casino's rooftop, taking a moment to enjoy the simple beauty. This was his second time seeing the sky in as many days. Before that, it had been… well, he wasn't sure. He and his wife, Sirena, had been holed up inside the building since the beginning. With the windows and doors boarded over, there had been no way to mark the passage of time – no switch from daylight to darkness. It had to have been at least a month. Maybe more. Yesterday, after what felt like several days of silence from the outside, he'd ventured out onto the rooftop, but he'd been too wired and cautious to bask in the view, focused instead on whether or not a dead thing – perhaps a human being or a bird – would try to eat him. There were plenty of corpses, for sure, but to Andy's surprise, rather than attacking him, they'd behaved like dead things were supposed to – motionless and rotting.

Worried it might be a fluke, or some kind of new zombie trick, he'd gone back inside and told Sirena they would wait another day. When he'd woke up this morning, rising from the makeshift bed they'd fashioned out of towels, tablecloths, and casino uniforms, he'd crept out of the vault and through the quiet casino floor until he'd reached the ladder to the roof. Then, armed with the SIG Sauer P365 9mm handgun he'd found on a dead security guard (Andy's own guns were back home in Yakima), he'd returned to the roof again.

The wind shifted, ruffling his white hair, and the stench of decay grew stronger. Wincing, Andy turned his attention away from the sky and back to the task at hand. He heard a faint buzzing and realized after a moment that it was flies. They were probably all around him, crawling over the buffet of bodies. He walked to the edge of the roof, taking care to step over the bird carcasses, and surveyed the countryside. The parking lot was littered with corpses, and pieces of corpses – human and animal alike. Some of them he'd put down before he and Sirena had managed to secure the building. Others had fallen during two different firefights that had taken place outside. During both of those events, he and Sirena had huddled in the darkness, waiting to see who would win. In both cases, he assumed the zombies had been the victors, as no survivors had tried to breach the casino's barricades. Both a large neon sign for the casino, and a smaller sign beneath it that advertised their Mystery Envelope Drawings, were splattered with blood, now dried brown. Andy wondered how the hell blood had managed to splash that high.

He paused long enough to clean his smudged eyeglasses on the hem of his shirt, and then he eyed the trees around the parking lot warily, expecting them to be filled with undead birds, but nothing moved among the branches. Farther away, the highway was empty as well, save for a three-car pile-up along one shoulder. The breeze shifted again, bringing a hint of smoke. Something was on fire somewhere, but he saw no sign of it on the horizon. Then the smell of decay returned, as did the buzzing of the flies.

"Is it over?"

Even though he recognized Sirena's voice right away, Andy still jumped, startled. He wheeled around, nearly dropping the handgun.

"You scared the shit out of me!"

"I'm sorry." Sirena giggled. "I thought you heard me."

Andy shook his head. "I wasn't paying attention. Lost in thought, I guess."

Sirena took one hesitant step forward. "Is it safe?"

Andy shrugged, relaxing. "I think so. It feels weird to say that. Like it can't be real. But I guess a year ago, I wouldn't have thought zombies were real, either. Now…?"

"Normal feels unnormal," she replied.

"Yeah. That's a good way of putting it."

She crossed to him, and they embraced. When she tried to kiss him, Andy tried to pull away. Sirena held him tighter.

"I haven't brushed my teeth in weeks," he said.

"So? Neither have I. And I can't remember the last time either of us showered."

"Point." He relaxed again and kissed her. He buried his face in her hair, breathing deep. "One thing's for sure."

"What's that?"

"Even without a shower, you still smell better than the zombies."

She broke the embrace and playfully shoved him. "You're terrible."

A mosquito flitted between them. Andy batted it away with his hand.

"So, what's the plan?" Sirena asked. "Are we going to stand out here wasting time?"

Grinning, Andy stared at his wife, thinking back to the eighties, when they'd gone to the prom together. He'd been a senior and Sirena was a sophomore. After graduation, he'd joined the Marine Corps and served onboard the USS Carl Vinson. They'd spent the next twenty-five years living separate lives and in separate marriages, often thinking of one another, but never reconnecting. In their time apart, Andy had two kids, his daughter Angela and his son, David. Sirena also had two children, her son Jacob, and her daughter Logan. Finally, nearly three decades after high school, they had reconnected via Facebook. At the time, each was married, but not very happily. They decided it would be best just to remain friends, as before. A year later, they'd reconnected again to discover each had separated from their respective spouses. A year after that, Andy made the trek from California to Yakima, Washington and moved in with Sirena. Marriage soon followed.

"This isn't wasted time." Andy's voice was thick with emotion. "No day with you is wasted."

Sirena opened her mouth to reply, but then kissed him again. Her eyes welled with tears.

"I love you," she murmured.

"I love you, too."

They stood quietly for a moment, until another mosquito buzzed them. This time, instead of simply batting it away, Andy swatted it to the rooftop and then stepped on it, crushing the insect beneath his foot.

Sirena sighed. "Seriously, though. What do we do now?"

"If I-82 is still passable, then it's about an hour and a half from here to Yakima. We can check on Logan. And the critters."

In addition to their daughter, the couple had two dogs and four cats in Yakima.

Sirena's expression hinted at conflicting emotions.

"What's wrong?" he asked.

"Do you... do you think...?"

"Logan's a smart kid. Tough, just like her mother. She's alive."

Sirena let out a deep, shuddering breath.

"We'll get her, and then head to Cheney and find Jacob. His roommates, too. And then we'll just cruise down the coast until we get to California, where we can pick up David and Angela and the grandkids. And then we'll all road trip to Vegas."

Andy struggled to keep his expression jovial. He was a realist. He knew that the odds of their kids, grandchildren, and pets still being alive were grim, but he wanted to keep Sirena's hopes up. And, he supposed, his own hopes as well.

"We always wanted to go to Vegas," he said. "Now we've got the time. All the time in the world."

Sirena wiped away tears, and pointed at their car, still sitting in the parking lot, now covered in dirt and gore. "We're not going to fit everybody in that."

"Then we'll get an RV. I'll bet there are—"

Andy paused, frowning. Sirena's expression had faltered again. She stared at the parking lot, eyes wide. He turned to see what she was looking at, and then he frowned, as well.

The grass between the tree line and the pavement was moving as if alive, each individual blade swaying back and forth. The trees had begun to do the same. It was then that he realized the wind had ceased. They moved of their own volition.

"What the fuck?"

From the direction of the highway, a dark shadow scurried toward the casino, sweeping over everything in its path. It wasn't until they reached the parking lot that Andy realized what they were – millipedes and centipedes. Tens of thousands of them.

"Andy." Sirena's voice was tinged with panic.

As he turned toward her, he caught a flicker of movement out of the corner of his eye. He glanced down at the squashed mosquito and gasped. The crushed insect twitched and wiggled. Then, slowly – horribly – the mangled corpse took flight. It rose unsteadily into the air, bobbing and weaving. Sirena recoiled. Andy raised his hand to strike the bug again, but paused, noticing something odd. Instead of biting them, the mosquito launched itself at a fly crawling atop the corpse of a bird. As he watched, the insect speared the fly with its proboscis.

"It…" He turned to Sirena. "It's not over. It's the bugs now. It's gotten into the bugs!"

If she heard him, Sirena didn't acknowledge it. Her attention was focused on the wriggling army blanketing the space below. They swarmed over the abandoned cars and everything else in their path. The two of them watched with growing dread as the creatures approached the building.

Something bit Andy on the neck. He slapped at it and then glanced down at his palm. Another mosquito lay spread out there, smeared across his skin. He whirled around and checked on the fly. Its attacker was gone, and the fly lay motionless. Then, as he watched, it began to twitch.

He grabbed Sirena's arm and showed her his palm. "This was the same one. They're not just going after other bugs. They're going after us, too. They're trying to finish the job!"

She gestured wildly at the ground below. "Shoot them!"

Andy let out a startled, choking laugh. His wife had never been comfortable with firearms, but she'd grown to tolerate them in the house over the years. Now, here she was encouraging him to use one.

He shook his head, tugging her arm. "Bullets aren't going to do any good against those. Come on!"

As they ran for the door, the air began to buzz. Within seconds, dozens of tiny forms began darting at their faces, targeting their eyes, noses, and mouths. Andy stumbled, nearly falling, but Sirena reached out and steadied him.

"This way," she urged.

Arms flailing, they reached the opening and hurried inside. Andy yanked the door shut behind them. The buzzing continued from the other side. They stood there in the dark, panting, listening in horror as tiny insectile forms rammed against the obstruction.

"Downstairs," he whispered. "We'll hole up in the vault."

Nodding, Sirena clambered down the ladder. Andy

quickly followed. They hurried through the casino, rushing past the silent slot machines and empty tables. The doors and windows remained boarded and secure, but a skittering sound filled the space as thousands of centipedes and millipedes and other creatures scrambled up the sides of the building.

"Can they get in?" Sirena stared, wide-eyed.

"I don't think so," he lied.

They reached the vault door, and Andy ushered Sirena inside.

"Where are you going?" she asked.

"To get us some supplies. We might be in there a while."

"Hurry back!"

Nodding, he rushed off to the kitchen. It had been well-stocked before the Rising, and the two of them had rationed carefully, so there was plenty of water and non-perishables left. He stacked canned vegetables and snack foods atop a case of bottled water, and then made his way back to Sirena. As he reached the vault door again, he heard glass shattering on the other side of the barricade. Andy quickly sat the supplies down on the floor and then closed the door behind him, making sure it was sealed. Then he sat down on the floor next to his wife and put an arm around her.

"There we go. All sealed in, nice and tight."

"And they can't get in?"

"This was the most secure room in the entire place. All the cash and stuff they had in here? Nothing's getting through that door."

He glanced up at the air vent in the ceiling.

"Nope," he repeated. "Nothing's getting in here."

Sirena snuggled against him. Andy sat the handgun within reach on the floor.

"Andy, we can't just sit here wasting time. Tell me you have a plan?"

"I do." He glanced down at the pistol and then back up at the open vent. Then he kissed the top of her head and breathed in her scent. "And we're not wasting time. The only time we wasted was those years apart."

"Yes, but if we hadn't had those years we wouldn't be where we are today."

"In a casino's backroom vault?"

She laughed softly. "You know what I mean. We had to go through everything we went through to be the people we are now. The people who are together."

He nodded. "That's my point. Every day with you since we found each other again? None of it has been wasted time."

"Not even during the zombie apocalypse?"

"Not even now. Other than the bugs, this was a pretty good day. We got to see the sunrise together."

"I hope we get to see it again."

He stared at the vent as his fingers traced over the gun.

"We will. When we get out of here, after we get the family, we'll watch the sun come up over Las Vegas every day."

Sirena stiffened against him. "Do you hear that?"

"Just you breathing."

"I thought I heard something in the ceiling."

"That's just air in the vents. That's all. Now focus. Let's enjoy this time."

LAST EMBRACE

CURTAIN CALL, PART 1

LITORAL, Equatorial Guinea

Sadie Hartmann was so focused on tuning out Jeremy that she almost didn't notice the heart-shaped rock sticking up out of the sand.

Even before the Rising, Jeremy had always been a talker, particularly if the conversation involved something he was enthusiastic or knowledgeable about. But the frequency of his talking had risen along with the dead, to the point where it was now some sort of verbal tic. Sadie supposed it was brought about by post-traumatic stress, although she wasn't sure that "post" was the operative word, since their traumas continued mercilessly, day after day. Traumatic stress, without the post, seemed more apt. Privately, Sadie acknowledged that she was suffering from it as well. In her case, she'd simply stopped thinking about her husband and their three children. She didn't think of them as dead, even though they were. No question about that. She'd seen each of them torn to pieces.

And so, in order to not remember that, she just didn't think of them at all. In her mind, they had simply never existed.

Which was why spotting the rock made it hurt all the more. It reminded her of her husband. Reminded her of...

Gasping, Sadie clutched a hand to her chest. Her vision grew hazy from a sudden welling of tears, and her lungs and throat ached. She bent over, scooped up the stone, and held it in her palm.

She closed her eyes.

She heard her husband's screams. Heard her children's shrieks. Heard the wet, ripping sounds... noises she'd never known a human body could make.

Sadie opened her eyes again and, in a flash of rage, flung the rock far out into the ocean.

"Pretty hard to skip a stone in that surf." Jeremy raised a hand to shield his eyes from the sun's glare. "Anyway, like I was saying, once we hook up with Jarod and his boat, we can make it to the Zafiro Producer, and then we'll be..."

"Jeremy." Sadie turned to him, interrupting. "You need to stop."

He frowned in confusion. "Stop what?"

"Stop with this talk of still following Jarod's plan."

"It's a good plan," Jeremy argued. "The Zafiro Producer isn't just any normal oil rig, Sadie. It's a floating fucking fortress. Once we reach it, we can—"

Sadie shoved him with both hands. Surprised, Jeremy teetered backward on the sand.

"Hey!"

"I don't want to hear about it anymore," Sadie shouted. "You and this fucking oil rig! We've traveled halfway across the fucking planet on a wild goose chase. Everyone

THE RISING

MORE SELECTED SCENES FROM THE END OF THE WORLD

ART GALLERY

ILLUSTRATIONS BY
CHARLIE BENANTE

ADDITIONAL ILLUSTRATIONS & COVER BY
WES BENSCOTER

SOPHIE

PLAN D

BUNKER HILL

GUNNER

HELL OF AN EARTH

SAFETY FIRST

ZOMBIE BUGS

WALK AMONG US

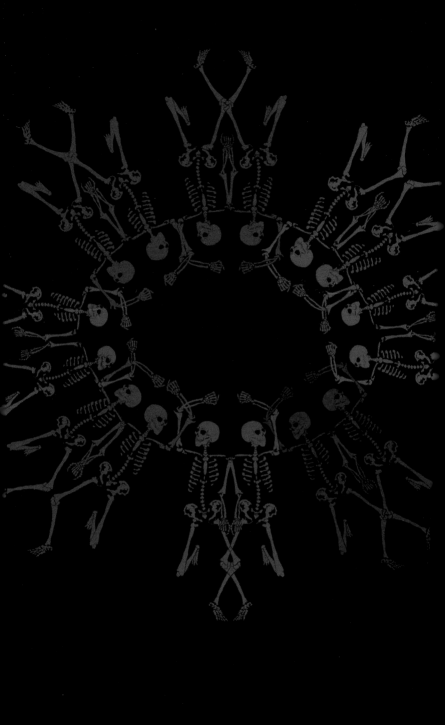

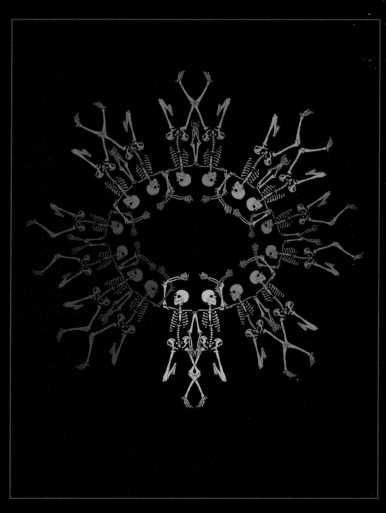

CAUGHT IN A MOSH

EVOL

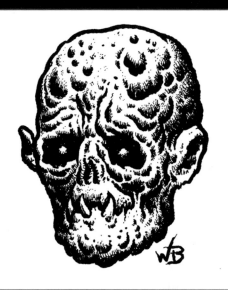

we know is dead! Do you understand that? My family is dead. Your wife is dead."

Jeremy's expression turned sad for a moment, but then he grew animated again. "But Jarod said if we got to the Zafiro—"

"Jarod is probably dead," Sadie interrupted again. "If he's not, then he's undead."

"You don't know that."

"And you don't either! Where is he?" She gestured toward the small town sitting just a few hundred yards further inland. "He hasn't come out to find us."

"He might not know we're here, Sadie."

"You don't think that maybe our plane crashing into the fucking ocean would alert him to the fact that we've arrived?"

Frowning, Jeremy glanced down at his feet. "Maybe he's on the rig already."

"And maybe he's in rock and roll Heaven with Kurt Cobain!"

Jeremy met her gaze again and shook his head. "Jarod wouldn't be hanging out with Cobain. He'd be wherever Dimebag Darrell is."

Sadie stared at him. Another burst of grief welled up inside of her, but this time it was for Jeremy's mental state. At some point between the moment that swarm of locusts had forced their private jet to crash and now, he'd finally snapped.

"Jeremy..." She sighed. "Listen to me, okay? That oil rig is no safer than anywhere else on Earth."

"You don't know that."

"And you don't know that it is!"

"Keep your voice down," Jeremy warned. "You want every corpse in the jungle to know we're here?"

Sadie gestured wildly at the spot where their wreckage had sunk beneath the waves. An oil slick spread across the surface. "Hello? Plane crash? That explosion was like ringing the dinner bell! If there were any zombies around, they'd be on us by now."

Jeremy took a deep breath, opened his mouth to speak, and then closed it again. He turned and began to trudge across the beach, heading toward the town.

Sadie frowned. "Where are you going?"

He shrugged, without looking back. "To find Jarod. He knew we were coming. He said he'd take a boat from the rig and meet us here."

"And he's not here! You're not going to find him."

"Then I'll find someone else. Anyone. Something. Aren't you tired of being alone, Sadie? We need to find other people. Humans aren't meant to be alone like this."

"Jeremy!"

He didn't pause and didn't look back. If he replied, she didn't hear him.

Sadie watched him go, but she did not follow. Instead, a wave of exhaustion swept over her. Lightheaded, she dropped to her knees. Her dirty, tattered shirt – stained with the blood of countless people and animals – hung loosely due to her rather startling weight loss. It hadn't occurred to her to find a replacement. It hadn't occurred to her to do much of anything, other than run, hide, and survive.

What are we doing, she thought. *What's the point of all this? We've seen four other living people in the last month, and all of them died in the plane crash.*

She felt like she was just going through the motions at this point. Was her continued survival based on some deep-seated primal instinct, or was it just luck? Did she really want to die? Perhaps secretly? Subconsciously? Was that what she'd been doing all along? Just hanging around, waiting for something to kill her?

No, she decided. *If I wanted to die, then I'd pick up a gun and shove it in my mouth and pull the trigger.*

What she really wanted was a hug. A simple human embrace. She and Jeremy hadn't engaged in that. She wasn't sure why. Maybe it was their shared trauma, or a sense of loyalty to their departed loved ones. Or perhaps it was because they hadn't really had a moment to let their guard down since this whole thing began. But that was what she needed. If she really was just hanging around, waiting for the end to come, then she'd like to feel a friendly embrace – a bit of human contact – before it arrived.

Her sadness turned to guilt. She could have been nicer to him just now.

Groaning, she clambered to her feet and brushed sand and dirt from her pants. Then she hurried after her friend. Jeremy had disappeared from sight, but she figured he couldn't have gone far.

As she jogged across the beach, she spotted the unmoving remains of a few zombies. One was human, one was a tiny monkey, and four were birds. All had rotted down to mostly skeletons and wore only a few weathered scraps of flesh. Curiously, none of them appeared to have suffered head trauma. She wondered if there was some other way to kill zombies that she and Jeremy didn't yet know about.

She reached the edge of the sand, and clambered onto a short, rough-hewn boardwalk. More decomposing bodies lay scattered before her, and as she craned her head, studying the sidewalks, alleys, and streets, she saw even more of them. There were plenty of humans, but also lots of native wildlife, including four huge gorillas and a hippopotamus carcass. The horrific stench was unbearable. After so much time fighting the dead, Sadie had become used to the smell, but it seemed overwhelmingly concentrated here. Sadie gagged as her stomach convulsed.

"Jeremy?"

Her voice sounded very small in the stillness.

Where is he, she thought. *He couldn't have gone that far. It's only been a few minutes.*

She padded forward, stepping over the rotting remains of humans, animals, and birds. Again, she noticed that none of them had any head trauma. It was almost as if the zombies had just laid down here and died. As she passed by the massive hippo carcass, she noticed a host of flies crawling through an open cavity in its side. Wrinkling her nose and nearly retching, Sadie hurried past.

She was about to call out for Jeremy again when she heard a buzzing noise behind her. She whirled around and saw the flies rising as a group from the bloated corpse.

"What the hell?"

Moving as one, the flies swarmed toward her. The noise they made was surprisingly loud.

Screaming, Sadie turned and ran, arms flailing around her face and head. She smashed several of the insects between her palm and cheek, and when she glanced down at her hand, her eyes widened in alarm. The squished flies were still moving, trailing their guts across her skin.

The insects were coming back from the dead now, just like everything else had before.

She fled, heedless of direction or her surroundings. The only sound on the deserted streets were her footfalls, her shrieks, and the incessant buzz of her pursuers. She spotted an open doorway in a storefront and veered toward the building. Sadie burst through the entrance and plunged ahead into the shadows. Something brushed against her face. Then another. She skidded to a halt. It was spiderwebs. Cringing, she turned and batted, trying to free herself, but instead, she only tumbled further into the space until she was covered.

As her eyes adjusted to the gloom, the walls, floor, and ceiling began to move.

No, she realized. *That's not it.*

The interior swarmed with spiders. Thousands of them scampered and scurried in the dark. Common house spiders, black widows, crab spiders, huntsman spiders, jumping spiders, and dozen more species that she couldn't identify. All of them converged on her, crawling up her legs and landing in her hair. Sadie was afraid to scream, because if she opened her mouth, they might get in. Instead, she whimpered, moaned, and sobbed as they began to spin, and bite, and spin some more.

After a while, her fears subsided. The tightening, thickening cocoon of webbing felt very much like an embrace. It was comforting, almost.

For the first time in a long while, Sadie allowed herself to remember her husband and children as they were when they were alive, rather than how they had died. She closed her eyes as they began to swell from the venom, and her lips pulled back in a smile.She hung around and waited to die.

GOREHOG

CURTAIN CALL, PART 2

LITORAL, Equatorial Guinea

Jeremy Wagner plunged through the streets, searching for Jarod or anyone else who was still alive. Instead, he found only the dead. The roads and sidewalks were littered with the corpses of humans and animals – men, women, and children, and also monkeys, birds, two panthers, a tiger, and a hippopotamus. The stench was cloying and horrific, but he barely noticed. Instead, Jeremy focused on the bodies themselves. Given the level of decay, he was pretty sure they had all been zombies, but the only way to kill a zombie was to damage its head, and none of the corpses showed any sign of head trauma. It was as if whatever had been animating them had simply vacated the premises, leaving the remains to collapse onto the ground.

He stopped for a moment and closed his eyes. The heat seemed to settle over him like mist. He opened his eyes again and winced, now aware of the smell. He put one hand over his nose and turned around to check on Sadie, but she wasn't there. Jeremy frowned. He was sure that she'd been right behind him. How far had he walked?

"Sadie!"

His shout echoed through the deserted town. It was the only sound, other than the incessant buzzing of the flies crawling and skittering over the dead.

Jeremy's frown deepened. He knew there was something wrong with him, and it wasn't just because of the plane crash. He'd been having trouble remembering things. It had started shortly after the Rising began, back when his wife... when she was... she...

He could no longer remember her name. She'd been his rock. His one sole focal point in the entire goddamned universe and he could no longer remember her name or how she had looked, because when he did try to remember, all he saw was her blood, and all he heard was himself screaming her name until his throat was so raw. As a result, he'd blocked her memory from his mind. But now, standing amidst the ruins of a small town on the African continent, just an hour after surviving a devastating plane crash, Jeremy began to wonder if that had been the healthiest approach to surviving.

He saw how Sadie had looked at him in the weeks past. She thought he was losing his mind.

She was probably right.

He balled his fists at his sides and purposely tried to remember his wife's name.

And found that he couldn't.

"Fuck."

He said it quietly, but his voice still echoed. The buzzing insects grew louder.

He remembered playing guitar in Broken Hope. Remembered every album and song they'd ever recorded.

Remembered all the crowds and stadiums they'd played, all over the world. He remembered Joe and Ryan and other friends lost along the way.

But everything after the Rising was just a jumbled fucking blur.

Indeed, as he stood there thinking, he realized that the plane crash was now a blur, as was Jarod's plan for them to meet up on the... what was it again? The Zafiro Producer?

"Losing my shit," he muttered. "Fuck this. I've got to get it together. Find Sadie."

He glanced around, trying to determine where Sadie might be, and was struck again by the eerie silence. It was so strange to be standing in the open without zombies running after him or shooting at him. If it weren't for the flies, he'd think he was the last living thing in the town.

Jeremy turned left and strode down the sidewalk, stepping over bodies every few feet along the way. The buzzing sound grew louder behind him. When he turned around, he saw clouds of flies, mosquitoes, and other flying insects rising from the corpses and following in his wake.

"What the hell?"

Moving as one, they drew closer, trying to surround him. Jeremy stumbled backward and ducked into a nearby bar. The insects followed, filling the doorway with their presence. The interior was unlit and stank of cigarette smoke and stale beer and decay. Not daring to look away from the bugs, he retreated further into the bar. His hip collided with the edge of a table, sending bottles crashing to the floor. They exploded in a shower of broken glass, but the insects pressed ahead, undeterred.

Jeremy drew a breath to yell again for Sadie, but when

he did, several flies and mosquitoes darted forward and tried to fly into his gaping mouth. He swatted them angrily, smashing several against his shirt. When he glanced down at them, he saw that their crushed forms were still twitching. His eyes widened. Jeremy quickly wiped the moving insects on his pants leg. One of the dead flies tried to climb upward. Whimpering, he balled up a fist and pulped the remains.

He retreated to a small stage at the rear of the room. Babbling aloud, he clambered onto the stage and frantically looked for another exit. He saw one to his right, but the door was ajar, and cockroaches scurried through it, blocking out the sunlight. When Jeremy glanced out at the bar, he saw it filling with more insects. He was trapped. He took a few plodding steps toward the exit door, but the roaches barreled toward him, climbing overtop one another in their rush.

Jeremy looked around for a weapon, but the only things he found were an acoustic guitar and the stool it sat leaning up against. His stomach sank with the futility of using either of them. Sure, he could swing at them, bludgeoning and crushing his tiny foes, but he was vastly outnumbered, and the rest of the horde would be upon him in no time at all.

Sighing, he slumped down onto the stool and picked up the guitar. He plucked the strings at random and was surprised to find that the instrument was in tune. His hands were shaking so badly that the guitar thrummed against his palms.

He stared out at the dead insects as they darted through the air and scurried up the walls and across the ceiling and blanketed the floor and other flat surfaces. There were hundreds of thousands of them, and given how the sunlight was dimming, there were thousands more outside, clamoring to get in. In a way, it reminded him of the Czech crowd he'd once played for during the Brutal Assault Festival of 2014. The attendees for that open-air concert, which had taken place in an eighteenth-century army fortress, had numbered close to twenty-thousand people.

This crowd dwarfed them.

"Thanks for coming out." Jeremy's voice cracked. "I guess this is a curtain call."

The insects fell silent.

"This" Jeremy continued, "is a song from our album, Swamped In Gore. It's called Gorehog."

His fingers stopped trembling as soon as he began to play.

"Uuuhhh," Jeremy sang, "gore hog brings death. Tusks, soaked with warm blood. Immense pig of doom..."

He was surprised that he remembered the lyrics.

The horde swarmed the stage, and in the last few seconds before the insects filled his throat and nose, he remembered his wife's name, and how she had looked before the end.

Jeremy died smiling.

WATCHING IT BURN

LONG LEVEL, Pennsylvania

Carter went outside to watch the end of the world.

It was the first time he'd left the house since the whole crisis began. Some people had said it was a pandemic or some escaped lab-grown super virus. Others said the cause was supernatural. Carter hadn't given the cause much thought during his isolation. The whys didn't matter. What was important were the *whats*, and over the last few months, the *whats* were that anybody – or anything – that died subsequently came back from the dead as a vicious, murderous, reanimated corpse. To Carter's way of thinking, it didn't matter if it was a virus or a demon inside the dead. The only thing that mattered was keeping his loved ones safe from them.

And that one thing – that only thing that mattered – was something he had failed at every step of the way.

When martial law was declared, they'd sheltered in the attic of their home – Carter, his wife Fidelia, their teenage daughter Maya, their son Kyle, and his mother-in-law, Myrna.

Maya was the first to die. On the third night of the siege, when they still had electrical power and the phones still worked, she sneaked out of the attic and the house, leaving a note behind that she was going to meet up in the park with her boyfriend, and that she would be careful, and that she'd be back soon. She'd told the truth about that. The girl had returned home, alright. Except that she wasn't Maya any longer, and most of her throat had been torn out. Her head hung lopsidedly on what remained, but that hadn't stopped her from trying to kill them.

When Carter closed his eyes, he could still hear the sound the baseball bat had made as he hit her with it.

Myrna had passed next. Although they'd moved all of their food, water, and other necessities into the attic when they first sheltered in place, the power had gone out about two weeks into the crisis. That meant the small dorm room refrigerator he'd lugged up into the attic no longer worked, which in turn meant that there was no way to keep Myrna's insulin from going bad.

Eventually, the old woman slipped into a diabetic coma and died.

Something else woke up inside of her, but by then they had dragged her corpse outside of the attic and barricaded the door again.

When Carter closed his eyes, if he wasn't hearing the sounds the baseball bat had made against his daughter's skull, he could hear his mother-in-law's guttural, maniacal laughter as she clawed and pounded on the attic door, demanding to be let in.

Fidelia committed suicide the next day. She did it while Carter and Kyle were asleep. She left a note, explaining her reasons. Then she jumped out of the attic window and fell three stories head-first. Her short, startled scream as gravity took control was what woke him. He heard her hit the pavement without understanding what was happening.

That sound haunted him, just like the baseball bat and Myrna's cries did.

But at least she hadn't come back, like the others. It would have been hard for her to do so, given that her head resembled a squashed gourd.

Kyle went last, killed by a tree.

They'd thought that the crisis was over. They hadn't seen or heard a zombie in over a week. So, the two of them had ventured downstairs, and while Carter was rummaging through the kitchen cupboards, voraciously searching for crackers or chips or anything else they might have neglected to take into the attic with them, Kyle had opened the door and stepped out into the backyard. Carter called for him, alarmed, but by then the boy had crossed the grass to his sandbox.

And then the tree... the big oak tree that Fidelia had always been after him to cut down and get rid of before it fell over on the house.

The tree killed him, pulverizing the boy into a wet, red mess.

So, when the second sun appeared in the sunset, Carter went outside and stared up at it, heedless of zombies or trees or anything else. The second sun hung there in the southern sky, white and tinged with red. It grew bigger by the minute. Carter felt the heat rising all around him. Struggling to breathe, he sat down in the grass.

The last thing he saw before the second sun grew too bright to look at were countless figures flying out of it, spectral and fluid in shape, but decidedly humanoid. They swept down toward the earth, and then he realized – they weren't swimming out of the sphere.

They *were* the sphere.

As the oak tree burst into flame, Carter closed his eyes, and for the first time in months, he didn't hear the baseball bat or his mother-in-law or his wife's head exploding.

And moments later, as he burst into flame, his tears of joy evaporated on his sizzling skin.

ABOUT THE AUTHOR

BRIAN KEENE writes novels, comic books, short stories, and nonfiction. He is the author of over fifty books, mostly in the horror, crime, fantasy, and non-fiction genres. They have been translated into over a dozen different languages and have won numerous awards.

His 2003 novel, *The Rising*, is credited (along with Robert Kirkman's *The Walking Dead* comic and Danny Boyle's *28 Days Later* film) with inspiring pop culture's recurrent interest in zombies.

He has also written for such media properties such as *Doctor Who, Thor, Aliens, Harley Quinn, The X-Files, Doom Patrol, Justice League, Hellboy, Superman,* and *Masters of the Universe.* He was the showrunner for Realm Media and Blackbox TV's *Silverwood: The Door.*

From 2015 to 2020, he hosted the immensely popular *The Horror Show with Brian Keene* podcast. He also hosted (along with Christopher Golden) the long-running *Defenders Dialogue* podcast.

Several of Keene's novels and stories have been adapted for film, including *Ghoul, The Naughty List, The Ties That Bind,* and *Fast Zombies Suck.* Several more are in-development. Keene also served as Executive Producer for the feature length film *I'm Dreaming of a White Doomsday*.

Keene's work has been praised by *The New York Times, The History Channel, The Howard Stern Show, CNN, The Huffington Post, Bleeding Cool, Publisher's Weekly, Fangoria, Bloody Disgusting,* and *Rue Morgue*.

Keene also serves on the Board of Directors for the Scares That Care 501c charity organization.

The father of two sons and the stepfather to one daughter, Keene lives in rural Pennsylvania with his wife, author Mary SanGiovanni.

ABOUT THE ARTIST

CHARLIE BENANTE is an icon in the music world, best known as the drummer for Heavy Metal bands Anthrax and Stormtroopers of Death (S.O.D.). A pioneer of double-bass drumming, he is credited with creating and popularizing the blast beat in thrash metal and praised for his lightning-fast double kick technique.

Also an accomplished guitarist, he contributed lead guitar to S.O.D.'s Speak English or Die album as well as composing the majority of the music throughout Anthrax's discography alongside rhythm guitar player and band leader Scott Ian.

In addition to his musician duties, Benante is also a graphic artist and has created many of Anthrax's album covers and T-shirt designs.

When he's not making music or art, Charlie is probably drinking coffee. His love of the bean has led him to create three blends with Chicago's Dark Matter Coffee.

Outside of Anthrax, Charlie is an obsessive collector–paraphernalia and rarities from *The Simpsons, The Nightmare Before Christmas,* and *Star Wars,* as well as a scaled-down replica of the shark from *Jaws.*